PLAYING DEEP
By Amanda Love

This book is dedicated to my wonderful family. Love you to the Moon and back.

PROLOGUE

My father is on the warpath again. I'm not sure what I've done this time but whatever it is, I know I'm in for a beating.

Unless I can find a place to hide.

"Where are you, you little fucker?"

I haven't had much time to check out all the potential hiding places in our new house yet, so I panic and crawl into the nearest - and most obvious - hiding place in the closet under the stairs. I pull the door closed behind me and wrap my arms around my knees as I sit in the dark, trembling, hardly daring to breathe.

The floorboards creak as he pauses outside the door and then continues past. I slump in relief.

Sometimes I can hide until he's calmed down and forgotten why he's angry with me.

And sometimes he finds me. Like today.

The door is suddenly flung open, nearly coming off its hinges as he drags me from my hiding place by my hair.

"Where is it, you little shit? His fingers dig painfully into my arms and he shakes me until I feel like my brain may be permanently damaged. "Where've ya hidden it!"

Before I can reply, he back-hands me. The force of the blow throws me into the opposite wall and I crumple to the floor. Pain explodes in the right side of my face and I taste blood in my mouth.

He grabs a fistful of my shirt and lifts me clean off the floor. He's a big man and I don't stand a chance against his superior strength. He pushes his face so close to mine that I can smell the fumes on his breath.

"Where. Is. My. Shit?" He enunciates every word, which is nothing short of a miracle as he's only been home from work an hour and has already burned his way through the half bottle that was left from last night.

I know better than to argue - it'll only end one way. "I know where it is. Put me down I'll go get it right now". I try not to let him hear the fear in my voice.

Thankfully, my words seem to appease him and he grunts and drops me back to my feet. "Make it quick!"

We've only been here a few days but I already know which grocery stores have a liquor license. If I run I can get to the nearest one and back in less than ten minutes. I grab my jacket - I'll need somewhere to hide the bottle.

Eight minutes later, I'm back with a full bottle of whiskey, breathing hard from exertion and adrenaline. I've stolen for him before - and for myself when the cupboards were empty of food - but each time it's getting a little harder. I've grown a lot over the last year which makes it harder to slip in and out unnoticed.

I take the bottle into the living room and find my father has already passed out in his chair, his mouth slack. He'll wake up here in the early hours of the morning and drag his sorry ass to bed - hopefully his - for a few more hours before getting up for work. I still don't know how he manages to hold down a job.

He moves from one casual job to the next, getting work when and wherever he can. He's managed to get work here as a laborer on a construction site. I guess it pays enough to cover the bills, feed his drinking habit and if I'm lucky, put a little food in my stomach. Once or twice I've wondered why he is the way he is but I've learned to keep my mouth shut and not ask questions.

Being careful not to disturb him, I leave the bottle on the table next to him and make my way to the bathroom.

I inspect the damage to my face in the mirror. I already have the beginnings of a nasty bruise over my right eye and my lip is split where I face-planted the wall.

He's done worse.

It's usually the belt across my back or legs so that the welts it leaves are hidden under my clothes. He got careless today, marking my face. I'll have to come up with a story about my 'clumsiness' for my new school on Monday. I can't risk what he'll do to me if anyone finds out.

I've been looking after myself since my mother left. For a while, I kept thinking she'd come back and get me but she never did. The anger and hatred I feel at her desertion has already started to hollow me out. I don't understand how a mother can leave her only kid with a madman. Although, I have to admit I don't feel like a kid anymore. I'm very different to other twelve-year-olds - I've had to be.

I clean myself up, splash water on my face and dab some antiseptic on my lip, wincing at the sting.

I'll heal.

Physically, at least.

TYLER

I park the Harley, cut the engine and remove my helmet, still straddling the bike.

My eyes wander to the front of the church and I grimace as the memories bombard me. It's been years. Too many and not enough. The pain is still there, burning like an acid in my stomach and a cancer in my brain.

Every Sunday morning my father would drag me here so he could spout his three Hail Mary's and repent his sins before we returned to our shitty life.

Fucking hypocrite.

I run my finger under the collar of my shirt. I hate suits and it doesn't feel right to be wearing one on the Harley. A Harley is meant for jeans and leathers.

A movement captures my gaze and I see her as she walks into the church with her father. She's the reason I'm here….and the reason I left in the first place.

Her long, dark hair is swept up into some fancy do, exposing the delicate sweep of her neck and jaw. Her dark brown eyes and pretty lips are seared into my brain. My cock springs to life as I remember those lips on mine - our first kiss had very nearly become our first time and the heat of those memories still has the power to bring me to my knees.

I take in her long legs and the shape of her exquisite ass in the form fitting skirt suit. Just looking at her from a distance gets me hard and I'm already imagining the things I'd like to do to her….with her.

She's always had this effect on me - she just never knew it.

Until one night five years ago. And then I left - without so much as a goodbye or even a note.

Five long years I've stayed away, giving her time to grow up and have the chance to make her own choices - even if those choices don't include me.

Five years spent running away from my feelings. I couldn't let her know back then - she deserved so much more than I could give her. She was too young and I was too fucked up. Maybe I still am.

I had to be here today. The day that she's burying her mother. It won't be easy - I'm pretty sure she hates me for leaving. But I'm back now.

Back to claim what's mine.

JENNA

The church is full of people who've come to pay their respects, a testament to the kind hearted and generous woman my Mom was.

The brain hemorrhage that robbed her of life so suddenly has taken her from us far too soon. Every death of a loved one is too soon. Our hearts are broken and our lives changed forever but I'm grateful that it was quick for her - that she didn't suffer.

I glance at my Dad who sits next to me at the front of the church, his face composed but pale. Mom's body lies just feet away in the oak coffin with a single red rose laid upon the top that Dad gently placed there earlier. His heart must be breaking in two - he's lost the woman he loved. His friend. His Wife. His lover.

My mouth lifts in a bitter little smile. I'd once thought I could have what they'd had together but that dream had also died a sudden death five years ago.

I'm lost in my grief as the priest begins the service. Words and hymns are a dull hum to my ears as tears spill down my cheeks and I say a silent goodbye to my Mom. Dad's own tears leave silvery streaks on his face and he reaches for my hand. He's not an overly demonstrative man so the physical contact is all the more poignant.

After the service, we file outside and her body is lowered into the ground to rest next to my grandparents. The priest says a few more words and I step forward, gently tossing another rose on top of her coffin to join the first.

Dad and I receive the condolences of fellow mourners in a blur of hugs and handshakes as people drift away, back to their own lives.

"I'll go get the car," Dad says.

"Okay. I'll just be a few minutes." My gaze is drawn back to the fresh earth covering the coffin at my feet.

Dad nods, "Take as long as you need."

I sink to the ground as the tears fall freely again.

"I always hated seeing you cry".

The familiarity of the deep timbre has my head snapping up, shock and disbelief sliding through my veins.

"Tyler?"

God, I hate how broken my voice sounds as his name escapes my lips. I'm torn between throwing myself into his arms or kneeing him in his soft and dangly parts.

He looks amazing. He's a beast of a man now, all broad shoulders and overwhelming masculinity in a sharp gray suit - a far cry from the boy I first met with a black eye and a split lip.

Feeling at a disadvantage, I rise to my feet, smoothing my skirt down with shaking hands. He's even taller than I remember and towers over me despite the heels I'm wearing.

His blond hair is neatly styled, replacing the over-long, careless way he used to wear it. My fingers itch as I recall what it was like to run my fingers through that hair, how his mouth felt on mine after so many years of loving him silently. A spiral of desire unfurls in my lower belly and lands between my legs as the memories of the last time we were together assault me.

I clench my teeth and school my features to hide my weakness. I'm loathe to admit that deep down, there is a part of me that has yearned for him today, on the day that my Mom has been put in the ground.

We've always there for each other - since I was ten and he was twelve.

And then five years ago he just up and left without a word. I'm trying to hold onto the pain and anger that thought brings.

"Why the hell are *you* here?" It's more of a statement than a question. I very rarely curse and the fact that I do so now shows how off balance I am.

I'm unprepared for his answer as his blue eyes bore into mine.

"I came back for you".

TYLER

God, she's beautiful!

All long, silky hair, rounded curves and flashing brown eyes. A flush now covers her previously pale complexion and her tits are rising and falling magnificently with her breathing. I want to bury my face in them, in her hair, her sweet pussy until she comes apart in my arms.

I stuff my hands in my pockets to disguise the fact that my dick is trying to escape in her direction. Man, I'm gonna need some serious shower time later!

Despite my body's demands and my earlier words, I need to take this slow. She's not going to trust me straight off the bat after the way I left.

"I'm sorry about your Mom," I pin her with my gaze, "I loved her too." That much is true. From the age of twelve, Maggie Danvers had been more of a mother to me than my own.

My excuse-for-a-fucking-father had alternated between hitting the whiskey bottle and hitting me and my mother. After she left, my father's unpredictable temper had turned to me in full force. I would never, ever forgive her for leaving me there, for not taking me with her. Her desertion has burrowed deep and festered.

Day after fucking day I endured my father's swinging moods and fists. Mostly, he hit me where it wouldn't show. Couldn't possibly afford to draw any more attention to the saintly father who was bringing up his son single-handedly when his wife ran out on them. What a fucking joke! He'd been a functioning alcoholic with a mean streak and a vicious temper behind closed doors.

The weights room and high school football had been my salvation. It was the perfect combination to vent my aggression. I had a real passion for football and was a natural in defense. I went from a scrawny kid to a force to be reckoned with in less than a year and by the time I was fifteen, I was bigger than my old man.

One night, he'd swung for me in a drunken stupor, as he'd done a hundred times before, but I was too quick and too strong by then. He never even saw the punch that split his nose open and unleashed a stream of blood down his chin. It was the last fucking time he ever tried to lay his hands on me.

I'd been gone a year when the cops found him after a call from a concerned parishioner who'd missed him at Church. He was sitting upright in his chair, where he'd been for days, an empty whiskey bottle at his feet. The death certificate said massive heart attack. It had been too kind a fate for the bastard as far as I was concerned and I'd felt nothing but relief at the news of his death.

No power on earth could have dragged me back for his funeral….I'm not sorry he's dead and I'm not about to pretend I am. I don't give a shit what people think - they have no fucking idea what he put me through.

But I had to come for Maggie's funeral.

And for Jenna.

Her eyes are still flashing fire in my direction and she ignores my earlier statement, going straight for the kill. "Why did you leave?"

I take a step closer and her fresh womanly scent wraps around my nostrils and makes me hard enough to poke a hole in the church wall behind me. I know somewhere infinitely softer and warmer that I'd like to sink my aching cock.

"I had to," I reply.

"You had to? That's the best you can do?" Her voice is laden with disbelief. "You were my best friend!"

I almost flinch at her use of the word "friend". I'm hoping to change that.

But right now, she's on a roll.

"Do you know what it did to me when you just up and left without a word? I didn't know where you were, why you left or if you were even still alive! Didn't I deserve more than that - after everything we'd been through together?" Her voice steadily rises and she's almost shouting by the time she's finished, her posture ramrod straight, her lithe figure vibrating with anger.

Fuck, she's glorious when she's angry!

I'd do anything right now to go back to that night five years ago and give it a different ending.

Yeah.

Right.

Who the hell am I trying to kid? I had nothing to offer her back then. Nothing but a shitload of baggage and dead-end prospects.

But that's not true not anymore. I might just be worthy of her now. The eighteen-year-old who left here certainly hadn't been. Her father had thought so too.

I take a step forward, closing the gap between us and before she comprehends what I'm up to, she's in my arms and my mouth is on hers.

She tastes just like I remember and I groan as my tongue sweeps across her closed mouth, demanding entry. For a few seconds, I think she's going to resist me and then suddenly she opens up, allowing me access to the honey inside.

Sweet. So fucking sweet!

I feast on her mouth as my hands grip her hips and pull her against my throbbing cock. Our tongues tangle and she moans and the sound almost has me shooting my load right then and there.

So much for taking things slow.

JENNA

I'm breathing hard as I tear myself away from the temptation of him and take a step back, putting some much-needed distance between us.

Tyler's managed to obliterate those years apart with one kiss. My breasts feel heavy and I can feel my nipples pressing against the thin material of my blouse as a pool of heat gathers between my thighs.

My body is betraying me even as my mind rebels.

"You can't just show up here, kiss me and expect everything to be okay!" I cross my arms over my chest in an attempt to hide the reaction of my body.

"I never expected to," Tyler admits.

"Why?" I ask the question again. "Why did you leave?" I *need* to understand why he left me so suddenly. "Was the thought of you and I so scary?" This thought has haunted me for the last five years.

He closes his eyes as if in pain. "God, what a fucking mess!" His eyes open and his beautiful blue gaze holds me in place. "There's so much I want to say to you, but not here, not now." He rakes his hand through his short hair as if he's forgotten that it's no longer the unruly mess it used to be.

The sound of approaching footsteps interrupts before I can reply.

"Jenna? You okay? I was beginning to wonder where…..," Dad stops abruptly when he sees who I'm with. "Tyler?" His eyebrows rise in surprise.

"Sir." Tyler dips his head towards Dad but the two men make no attempt to shake hands.

"What are you doing back here?" Dad asks. I'm sure I must be imagining the almost accusatory edge to his question.

"Came to pay my respects," Tyler replies, his eyes flicking towards the freshly covered grave. "Maggie was a special woman."

"Shame you didn't show your own father the same courtesy." Dad's eyes are narrowed.

"Dad!" I'm shocked at his sudden antagonism.

Tyler looks as if he's ready to explode, barely containing his temper as his fists clench at his sides.

"With all due respect, *sir*," he coats the words with sarcasm, "that's none of your fucking business!"

"Still haven't lost that foul mouth of yours, I hear," Dad says. He turns his back, dismissing Tyler without a word. "We need to go, Jenna. I need to get home and pack."

I'd forgotten about Dad's business trip tomorrow after the events of today. His job as a football recruiter takes him away from home often, traveling to schools and sporting events all over the country to scout for up-and-coming sports talent. He's built a solid reputation with his sharp instincts, taking kids with raw sporting abilities and placing them in the right environment to grow their natural talent. Several of his kids have gone on to major league football success.

"Safe journey, Tyler," Dad gives him a curt nod as we turn to leave and I'm perplexed by the animosity I can feel rolling off both men.

"I'll be staying a while, sir," Tyler words sound like a challenge.

The two men stare at each other for a full minute and something unspoken passes between them. "I see," Dad says abruptly. "Let's go, Jenna." He turns on his heel and heads back down the path toward the car.

I turn to follow. The combination of Mom's funeral and Tyler's unexpected reappearance has left me needing to crawl away and lick my wounds.

"I'll be seeing you, Jenna." Tyler stands there, hands stuffed in pockets, all arrogant masculinity.

This time, his words sound like a promise.

TYLER

Shit!

I hadn't meant to kiss her but seeing her like that after so long had made my cock switch places with my brain. And she'd kissed me right back. It's far more than I expected and a glimmer of hope springs to life in my chest.

Watching her walk away from me now is the second hardest thing I've ever had to do. The first was leaving her five years ago. I want to call her back, take her in my arms again and make her mine in every sense of the word.

I need to play my cards carefully though. I can't afford to rush her, scare her away. I've got some time off before pre-season training starts and I have a feeling it's gonna take me every bit of that time to get her to trust me again. I won't be happy until she's under me and I'm buried shaft deep in her softness.

I head back to my Harley, climb on and fire her up. I vent a little of my frustration as I floor it and peel away from the sidewalk with a squeal of tires.

It doesn't take long to reach my hotel and check-in. I ignore the way the blonde receptionist's hand lingers a little too long on mine as she hands me my key card.

"If there's anything you need.....anything at all, don't hesitate to call me. I'm here all night," she purrs, her eyes walking up and down me like hands, hesitating at my crotch as she checks out the goods.

Her interest doesn't elicit so much as a twitch from my dick. There's only one pussy he's interested in - and it ain't hers.

"I've got everything I need, thanks." I leave her there without a backward glance and head up in the elevator.

Once in my room, I head straight for the bathroom, shedding clothes on the way and I'm naked by the time I reach the shower cubicle.

The powerful spray feels good on my body as I reach for the soap and lather up.

I conjure up her dark brown eyes, full lips, and beautiful tits and slide my hand up my instantly engorged shaft, resting the other against the shower wall in front of me. Her lips replace my hand as she swallows as much of my length as she can, her hands cupping my ass as she sucks and licks, driving me fucking insane.

"Oh God, Jenna!" I move both hands to the back of her head to hold her steady, sliding my cock in and out of her mouth as I go over the edge.

"Fuck, baby!"

My cum shoots over the shower wall before being washed away by the spray.

My breathing returns to normal as my fantasy evaporates and I'm alone in the shower again.

JENNA

I keep stealing glances across at Dad as we ride home in silence, puzzling over his reaction to Tyler.

It's not long before we're pulling up in front of our house and its familiarity warms me and makes me feel safe.

We live in a three bedroom single storey with a porch running the length of the front of the house and the proverbial white picket fence enclosing the front yard. Mom's plants have now blossomed with the early spring sunshine, adding splashes of color to the yard and porch, a poignant reminder that she was really here. If I close my eyes I can still picture her out front, her hands deep in the earth as she plants her beloved flowers.

I've heard people say that the memories of lost loved ones make it too painful to live in the same house after they're gone, but it's the opposite for me. It's a comfort feeling her presence in every room and sometimes I think I can smell the lingering scent of the fragrance she used to wear.

Once inside, I head straight to the kitchen, tossing my purse on the counter. "Coffee?" I ask Dad.

"I don't want you seeing him again."

I turn to face him, shocked by his words. "Tyler? Why? Not that it's your decision to make." I add.

"You, of all people, should know why." Dad replies. "I remember how broken you were after he left."

So *that's* the reason for the animosity toward Tyler! I'd tried so hard to pretend I was okay after Tyler left. I guess I hadn't done as good a job at hiding my feelings as I'd thought.

There's pain in Dad's expression and something more underlying it that I can't quite put my finger on.

"It's ancient history, Dad," I shrug. "I've moved on, got a good life, a great job." The words sound hollow even to my own ears.

It was true that I'd immersed myself in my job over the last few years. I decided to skip college after graduating high school to snap up a full-time opportunity at the leisure complex in town where I'd been working after school since I was sixteen. The job came with on-site training and the opportunity to learn the ropes from the ground up - something I couldn't pass up.

I love the work and enrolled myself on any and every training course I could, learning everything from staff management to social media to cash handling and budget control. My hard work over the last three years paid off recently when I landed one of the Deputy Manager positions, along with a decent pay rise.

"Really?" Dad continues, as I place two steaming cups on the kitchen table and we both pull up a chair. ""You work, eat and sleep - in that order. You don't date and you rarely go out and party like most young women your age. Wait - I can't believe I just said that!" Dad says with wry humor. "Most fathers would be happy that their daughters aren't out drinking and partying!"

He's not wrong. My job has left me little time or energy to socialize outside of my long hours. I have girlfriends, mostly colleagues from work who've become friends and we often lunch together, but most of them are in relationships or married with kids and none of us would qualify as party animals.

I drop my eyes to my coffee cup. "Things......weren't the same for me after he left. I guess he just didn't feel the same way about me that I felt about him." We both know I'm talking about Tyler.

Dad leans forward, resting his elbows on the table and dropping his head into his hands. He pushes his fingers through dark hair that's now sprinkled with gray.

"God, forgive me, I've made a mess of things!" he groans, looking at me with tormented eyes. "I thought I was doing the right thing - you were only sixteen, for Christ's sake!"

I'm shocked by Dad's sudden outburst and as he lifts his eyes to mine now, I recognize the emotions that I couldn't quite put my finger on earlier.

Regret.

And Guilt.

My heart stutters and then picks up at a faster tempo. "What do you mean?"

Dad sighs resignedly, looking weary beyond his years. "I'm the reason Tyler left."

His words don't make sense. "How can you be the reason?"

"I made him an offer he couldn't refuse."

I feel sick. "What offer?" My words are barely a whisper.

Dad can't look me in the eye. "You have to understand, honey, I was only trying to do what I thought was best for you!"

"What offer, Dad?" I'm almost shouting now as I repeat the question.

Dad looks at me for a few long seconds and then sighs, coming to some internal decision. "I'll tell you everything, honey, but I need you to hear me out until I've finished."

My stomach is roiling with nausea and it takes everything I have to keep my mouth shut and let him continue.

"I know I wasn't here as much as I should have been when you were growing up - my work has always taken me away from home a lot." He's not telling me anything I don't already know. Mom and I would have months on our own while Dad traveled the country.

"Tyler and his dad had been here several weeks when I got back from a trip," Dad continues. "I went over there to introduce myself - I wanted to meet the father of the kid you'd become attached at the hip to in my absence." His smile is weak.

"Tyler's father was out on the front porch when I got there - he'd just gotten home from work. He offered me a drink and we got talking. He told me about his wife leaving and what a struggle it was doing everything as a single parent. Tyler was a handful, he said. He wasn't doing well without a mother around and was getting into trouble and skipping school. Poor man seemed at his wit's end with what to do with him. I felt kind of sorry for the guy." Dad pauses and looks me straight in the eye. "But his son didn't sound like the kind of boy I wanted hanging around my daughter."

"If you felt that way then why did you let him come 'round?" I ask.

"Your Mom," Dad says simply. "She liked Tyler, said he was misunderstood and that he'd been nothing but polite and helpful all the times he'd been here. He'd eat here often and you were good for each other, she said. So I went along with it.....until the first time Tyler was arrested." Dad's mouth thins with disapproval. "I was all for making sure he never stepped foot in this house and you never saw him again. Your Mom disagreed. She always was a soft touch," his eyes mist over with memories, "but when she dug her heels in there was no changing her mind. I never understood why, but she fought his corner."

I had an idea why. My Mom had often seen things in people that others missed. She may have had her suspicions about Tyler's home life but there's no way she could have known the full extent of it.

"I watched him like a hawk when I was here," Dad says. "A few years later, when I came home after a few months away, I noticed the way he looked at you was......different. I could see you had feelings for him too, but you were barely sixteen and I knew it was only a schoolgirl crush." A blush creeps up my neck and into my face at the thought that my feelings had been so transparent. "I wanted better for my daughter than a kid with no prospects and a police record. So, I decided to take matters into my own hands."

"What did you do?" My voice is a whisper.

Dad pauses to take a sip of his coffee before continuing. "He didn't know it but I'd been watching him play football at high school. When I'm first scouting for new talent, I like to be discreet, see the potential of the kids in their home environment without the pressure of knowing someone is watching them. He was good. Really good. So, I pulled a few strings, got him a full-ride scholarship. It wasn't easy but I have a good reputation and great contacts. The only condition was that he got out of your life and left you alone, let you grow up and make something of your life without him. It didn't take much convincing to make him see that he had nothing to offer you, no real prospects," Dad has the grace to look a little ashamed as he says this. "Without my influence, no college would touch him. It's a miracle he graduated high school at all."

Rage bubbles up and lodges in my throat. "He graduated because I helped him," I say through clenched teeth. "Every day. For two years. But you wouldn't know that because you were never here!" I'm shouting now, so mad I could spit nails. "You have no idea what you've done!"

"What *I've* done? I put my reputation on the line! For you! Your future!" Dad's voice is raised now too. "It was a mutually beneficial agreement on both sides!"

I can't believe what my dad is saying. One of the people I trust most in the world has just devastated me. And he's calling it a *'mutually beneficial agreement?'*

"What you did," I snarl, "was emotional blackmail. Pure and simple! You destroyed one of the most important relationships in my life and all because *you'd* made up your mind that Tyler wasn't good enough me. You based your whole opinion of him on one lousy conversation with his father. God, what a joke that is!" I laugh humorlessly. "You don't know Tyler - you never did, never wanted to! You were never here long enough to really know him - or me for that matter!" I ignore the pain that flashes across his eyes, before plowing on. "You only saw what you wanted to see - you took what you thought you knew and put him in a tidy little box labeled "trouble" rather than take the time to really get to know him! You have no idea what his father put him through! The things he did to him!"

"What do you mean, what his father put him through?" Dad looks unsure now.

In my anger, I've said far more than I meant to, but I'm at the point of no return. I'm about to break a promise I made when I was ten years old. It's time my father knows just what he's done.

TYLER

I'm only half listening to the news on TV as I lay on the hotel bed. My thoughts keep straying to Jenna and how damned good she looked today.

She's filled out over the last three years, her tits are fuller, her hips and thighs all womanly curves and I want to taste every fucking inch of her. I opened a floodgate of pure lust when I kissed her five years ago and no woman has affected me in the same way since.

I groan, rolling onto my stomach, grinding my throbbing cock into the mattress. My shower time has done nothing to ease the eternal hard-on that just thinking of her produces.

My cell phone vibrates on the bedside table. I check the caller ID before answering, hitting the speakerphone button.

"Hey, Jake."

"Where are you, man?" Jake's voice rumbles over the phone.

"At the hotel," I reply.

"How'd the funeral go?"

"You know. It went."

"Yeah, man, I know." Jake pauses. "You still planning on staying a while longer?"

Jake knows the reason I've come back here. He's been a good friend and the only other person I've shared some of my shit with. Only some. There's only one person who knows all of it.

"Yeh. Gotta at least try." I reply.

"Do what you gotta do, Ty. Everyone deserves a little peace." That's a deep comment coming from Jake who's a complete man-ho and fucks his way through women like the world is on the brink of an apocalypse. His only criteria is that they're blonde and have a pussy. I wonder fleetingly about his blonde fetish but hey, who the fuck am I to pass judgment when my obsession has long, brown hair and dark eyes.

"You got that right," I reply. "Thanks for checking on me, Jake."

"Anytime. I'll catch up with you tomorrow."

I end the call and roll onto my back.

I need some sleep. I need to escape the memories that coming back here has unleashed………..

The bed depresses as his weight settles behind me. Every fiber of my being tenses, my body on red alert.

Not tonight! Please God, not tonight!

His breath is hot and heavy in my ear and the stench of his breath almost makes me vomit.

"Roll over!" he growls.

I roll onto my stomach as he uses one hand to rip my underwear down around my ankles and the other to pin me to the mattress. As he grunts above me I allow my mind to drift somewhere else. Anywhere else but here……

I wake in a cold sweat, gagging on the smell of whiskey in my nose and throat. There'll be no more sleep for me tonight. There never is after one of my nightmares.

I head for the shower. I need to scrub myself clean. I wish I could scrub the memories away just as easily.

JENNA

Sleep is elusive and I spend the night tossing and turning, replaying Dad's confession over and over.

Sometime in the early hours I hear Dad leaving for his trip and I feel relieved that I don't have to face him for a few weeks. I need time before I can look him in the eye again without hating him for what he did.

It had been strangely cathartic telling him the truth. Dad had looked physically sick afterward but I'd felt no sympathy for him. I know he's devastated by what I've told him but nothing will ever convince me that he'd had the right to manipulate mine and Tyler's lives like that.

I finally went to bed with the promises of him "making things right" after his trip ringing in my ears. Those are empty promises, as far as I'm concerned. The damage has already been done.

The hardest pill to swallow is that Tyler could've refused Dad's 'agreement'. He could have chosen to stay. Or I could have gone with him - I would have followed him anywhere if he'd asked. Whilst Dad hadn't known the truth of Tyler's home life, he had still played on Tyler's weaknesses, telling him that he'd never amount to anything so long as he stayed here.

And I can never forgive him for that.

So why has Tyler come back now? Was it only to pay his respects to Mom? And that kiss! My body heats as I recall how I kissed him back and a curl of lust spirals straight to my core.

I groan and turn over onto my stomach, punching my pillow in frustration. Whatever the motivation for his return, I won't risk my heart on him again.

I finally fall asleep, haunted by images of a boy with a bruised face and split lip …

"Take this over to our new neighbors, honey," Mom says, holding out a freshly baked pie towards me. "They won't have to worry about fixing up a meal if they're still busy unpacking."

I take the pie from her outstretched hands and she wraps a clean dish towel over the top. She has a smear of flour on her cheek and her long, dark hair is falling out of the loose ponytail she's tied it in. This thoughtful gesture is typical of Mom.

Our new neighbors have just moved into the house where Mr. & Mrs. Turner used to live. Mrs. Turner died and Mr. Turner can't look after himself anymore so he's gone into a retirement home.

I've decided I never want to get old.

We live in a quiet street outside of town with less than a dozen houses all spread out with a decent amount of land around them.

It's not far to walk and takes me less than five minutes to reach my destination. The house is unique in that it's set further back from the road than the other houses, giving it a little more privacy. It's in need of some attention with peeling paint and an overgrown yard. Maybe the new neighbors will clean it up and breathe fresh life into the old place.

As I head up the path I can see a boy sitting on the front porch, head bowed, arms swinging aimlessly between his legs. His head whips up as I approach, an almost feral expression on his face. His blond hair needs a good cut and curls around his neck. Startling blue eyes watch me carefully but it's his bruised face and swollen lip that capture my attention.

"What happened to your face?" I blurt, forgetting my manners with my curiosity.

"None of your fucking business," the boy growls.

I'm not easily intimidated but I'm still a bit taken aback by his aggressiveness. "I'm Jenna. I live over there," I choose to ignore his less than welcome response and point in the general direction of my house.

"What do you want?"

"Why are you so rude?" I throw the question straight back at him.

His eyes flash blue streaks of fire at me. "I don't like you," he almost spits the words. "Fuck off!"

Strangely, I'm not shocked or upset by his words. I have my Momma's instincts and they're telling me that there's more to this prickly boy than meets the eye. "You can't not like someone you've only just met."

"Wanna fucking bet?" he snarls.

"Wow, you really are Mr. Personality, aren't you? I say sarcastically. "Your loss," I shrug. "I'm actually a pretty cool person to know."

I suddenly remember I'm still holding the pie. "Momma made you this. She thought you might like it seeing as you've only just moved in and you're probably still busy unpacking," I give him my most insincere smile, "Careful you don't choke on it!"

I place the pie on the porch step at his feet, trying not to notice the expression of hunger that flickers over his face before he has a chance to hide it.

"You're welcome," I say at his lack of thanks. He glares at me. "Oooookay. Well….hope I don't see you around, then," I say chirpily, as I turn to walk away.

"Wait."

He says it so quietly I almost miss it. I turn back in surprise. "What sort?" I look at him in confusion. "What sort of pie?" he elaborates.

"Oh! Steak. It's a steak pie." I seem to be repeating myself. He looks at me for a few seconds as if he's making a decision.

"Wait here," he orders before disappearing into the house. He's back in no time carrying plastic plates and cutlery. "Sit." It doesn't sound like a request.

I try not to let him see how unsettled I am about the sudden turn of events. "Oh...um....I should really be getting back."

"Sit," he says again. "Please." It sounds as if it's painful for him to say the word. I get the feeling he doesn't ask for much from anyone and my heart softens a little.

I plonk down on the step next to him while he puts two huge helpings of pie on the plates. "Um...doesn't your Dad want some?" I'm worried there'll be none left at the rate he's heaping it on the plates.

His face closes up. "He's asleep. I'll save him some for later." He begins devouring his portion as if it's the first time he's seen food for days. I push my pie around on my plate, not wanting to admit that I've already eaten. "You gonna eat that?" He says through his last mouthful of pie.

I shake my head and hand him my plate, watching him tuck hungrily into my helping. "What's your name?" I ask.

He swallows another huge mouthful of pie before replying. "Tyler. My name's Tyler".

It's late morning when I wake. I panic for a moment thinking I'm late for work before remembering that I'm on annual leave for a few days following Mom's funeral.

I need to keep busy. Sitting around with my own thoughts isn't an option today. I need to let off some steam and decide to head over to Undercover Rock, the climbing center in town. I haven't been since before Mom died.

I developed a passion for indoor climbing after doing a training course for work a year ago. There's a climbing wall at the leisure complex where I work but they don't have a bouldering section, which is what I want to do today.

I dress quickly in leggings and a t-shirt with "Fight the Dead, Fear the Living" on the front. I stuff my feet into my sneakers and grab a protein bar before heading out the door.

Twenty minutes later I park my little Honda outside Undercover Rock, the large warehouse building that houses the climbing center. I grab my climbing shoes from the trunk and head inside.

After paying the entry fee I head to Urban Rock on the top floor which is dedicated to bouldering. I'm happy to see I have the place to myself - being a weekday it's much quieter than usual.

After warming up, I lose myself in the challenge of navigating the complex shapes, diverse angles and adrenaline of climbing without ropes. My stress melts away as my muscles stretch and burn, my only focus being where to find the next hand and foot hold.

"Nice grip you've got there!"

I'm so lost in my own world that the unmistakable voice behind me causes me to lose said grip and tumble to the ground.

TYLER

Jenna hits the crash mat with a thump.

"Shit!" I'm by her side in an instant. "Jen! You okay?" She's flat on her back, struggling for breath. "It's okay, you're winded," I reassure her. "It'll pass in a minute. Just try to relax." I stroke her hair back from her face where it's come loose from her ponytail. God, touching her feels good!

Her breathing is slowly coming back to normal and her eyes are now shooting sparks at me. I hold up my hands in mock surrender "I'm sorry. I really didn't mean to startle you like that."

Jenna pushes herself to a sitting position, then winces as she reaches around to rub her back. "I didn't hear you come in," She makes it sound like an accusation.

"Here let me see," I move behind her and push her hands out of the way, lifting her t-shirt. "Is this where it hurts?" I ask as my fingers gently knead her lower back. Her breathing hitches as my hands move on her warm skin and my chest swells with the knowledge that she's just as much at the mercy of her body's reactions as I am.

I catch a glimpse of her lace panties where her leggings have shifted with her fall and my cock instantly springs to life. I want to slip my hand inside those panties, into the soft wetness of her folds and rub her until she screams my name and releases her sweet juices all over my hand.

I'm suddenly thankful for the baggy sweats I'm wearing which go some way to disguising my enormous hard-on.

"It's fine now," her voice is husky as she pulls her t-shirt back into place and stands. I decide to let her go.....for now.

"Nice T-shirt," I indicate the slogan on the front. "You planning on a zombie-killing spree?" She smiles. It's the first time I've seen that smile in five years and it's the most beautiful fucking thing I've ever seen.

"You watch it?" she asks.

"Yeah, I watch it," I reply. "What's not to like about undead rotting corpses and a madman with a bat called Lucille." She laughs softly and I swear I could spend the rest of my life listening to that sound.

"What are you doing here?" she asks as if suddenly remembering where we are.

I decide that honesty is the best policy. "I came by your house and you were just leaving so I followed you here. I've been watching you for the last ten minutes." Her eyebrows lift in surprise. "I'm not stalking you." I think about that statement for a minute, "Okay, I guess I kind of am," I admit, giving her a rueful smile.

"Tyler....."

"Jenna, listen," I interrupt, pinning her with my gaze. "I know you're mad and hurt that I left the way I did but there are things I need to tell you, things you need to know." She doesn't speak, so I plow on. "Give me a few hours of your time to explain and if you still want me to leave after that I'll go and never bother you again." The thought of that kills me but I have to give her the option.

"Okay."

"Okay?" I can't believe it was that fucking easy! But I'm not about to question it and give her the chance to change her mind. "I'll pick you up tonight at eight." She nods.
As I turn to leave, I add, "Wear jeans."

JENNA

When I get home I take a long soak in the tub and wash and dry my hair so that it falls in soft waves down my back. As I stand in front of my mirror in my bra and panties I wonder if this is all a big mistake.

Tyler's confession that he'd followed me today has a flutter of hope stirring in my belly and the feel of his hands on my skin after my fall has me wanting things that I shouldn't. I didn't tell him about Dad's confession earlier because I need to hear his version of events. I only have Dad's side of things and even if it turns out I don't want to hear what Tyler's got to say, I have to give him the same opportunity.

I finish getting ready, choosing a pink fitted t-shirt and sliding into my jeans, wondering why he asked me to wear them. I'm just grabbing my sweater from the back of my chair when the doorbell rings.

Tyler is standing on the doorstep and holy-mother-of-all things-hot, he looks good! My hungry eyes travel upwards from his booted feet, jean clad legs and muscular thighs to the tight black t-shirt under a leather jacket.

My mouth is dry by the time my eyes reach his face and I realize that I'm on the receiving end of a thorough perusal of his own as his eyes travel up and down my body, lighting fires wherever they land.

He shifts uncomfortably and clears his throat. "You look beautiful."

"It's just jeans and a shirt," I reply, feeling self-conscious.

I lock the door and we make our way down the path. I'm halfway down when I spot the motorbike and his request for me to wear jeans becomes clear. "You got one," I say softly, looking up at him.

"Built it myself." he says. "Sold my truck and used some of the money from the sale of the house - seemed as good a way as any to spend it. He owed me that."

I reach up to touch his face and he closes his eyes, turning his mouth to kiss my palm. The simple caress sends a shiver down my spine.

The moment is broken as Tyler moves away abruptly, plucking a helmet from the top of the tank before turning to me and placing it on my head, making sure it fits properly. He removes his jacket and I get an eyeful of his bulging biceps and sinewy forearms as he holds it in front of me. I turn so that I can slide my arms into the sleeves and Tyler's scent envelops me. It's far too big but Satan and all his hellhounds couldn't rip this jacket from my body now.

Tyler reaches down between my legs, his hands brushing my inner thighs as he catches the edges of the jacket together and slowly zips it up. My heart goes wild and I almost lean into his hands, wanting to prolong the contact.

After putting on his own helmet he straddles the bike, flicking the kickstand up with his booted foot and indicating for me to slide on behind him. I loop my purse across my body and as I settle in behind him, I suddenly realize how intimately we're pressed together. The whole of my front is molded to his back as I slip my hands around his waist, feeling his stomach muscles clench. I tighten my thighs around the back of his hips to secure my hold on him as he starts up the bike.

"Hold on tight!" he yells over the throb of the engine and we're off with a screech of tires.

Tyler handles the bike expertly as we eat up the road, whipping around corners, and a feeling of exhilaration steals over me. After a few minutes, it dawns on me where we're headed and my heart jumps into my throat.

It doesn't take long to get there and before I know it, Tyler parks and cuts the engine in front of the lake.

Our lake.

Where he first kissed me.

Before I can dismount, Tyler swings his long legs around and swivels in his seat to face me, trapping my legs between his thighs. He removes his helmet before reaching forward to do the same for me. As if he can't help himself, he smooths my disheveled hair away from my face and our eyes lock.

"There's so much I need to tell you," he sighs, resignedly, "and you're not going to like it much. Your father......"

I place my fingers over his lips, stilling his words. "I know."

His eyes narrow, "You know?"

"Not until last night," I clarify. "When we got home after the funeral yesterday, Dad told me he didn't want me seeing you again." Tyler's jaw flexes but he remains silent.
"I didn't understand the animosity I felt between you both when Dad saw you at the cemetery." God, was it only yesterday that we buried Mom? It feels like a lifetime ago after all that's happened since. "I told him in no uncertain terms that he couldn't tell me who I could and couldn't see. He got upset, started talking about what a mess he'd made of things." I shrug. "Then he told me everything. About the scholarship."

Tyler is silent for so long that I begin to wonder if he's heard what I've just said.

"Fuck!" he suddenly explodes. "You must hate me!"

"I don't hate you, Ty," I say softly, "I could never hate you. I still remember the first time I met you," My mouth lifts in a small smile. "You were all fake bravado with a foul mouth. You were a fighter. You still are. Which is why it's so hard for me to understand why you didn't fight for *me*. For us."

His head goes back and his eyes close briefly as if in pain. "Because I knew I wasn't good enough for you. I knew it. Your father knew it. You were everything I wasn't - sweet and pure with a heart as big as the open skies. I was.....am......damaged goods." His words are laced with a bitterness beyond his years.

My heart breaks at his words. "You were always good enough, Ty. What happened wasn't your fault. You were surviving the only way you knew how in the worst situation imaginable. You can't let what your father did to you define you - you are so much more than that. I saw it the first time we met, the goodness in you that you tried to so hard to hide underneath all the hurt and pain. I saw it here," I touch his eyes, "and here," my hand moves over his heart.

Tyler groans and presses my hand against his chest. "You worked your way under every fucking one of my defenses," he recalls. "Only you. A slip of a girl with a braid down her back who came skipping up my path with a steak pie and a smart mouth, all soft eyes and even softer heart."

"Well, I did tell you I'm a pretty awesome person to know." I smile cheekily at him.

"I won't argue with that," he says huskily. He looks out over the lake, a far away look in his eyes. "The last time I brought you here I kissed you and before I knew it I'd stripped you to the waist and buried my mouth on you here," his blue eyes swing back to me and his hand moves up to hover over my breast, lingering but not touching. My breath is coming in short puffs as I remember too, my nipples tightening into hard nubs. I want nothing more than for him to close those last few inches and touch them, taste them like he had back then.

"I was kissing you goodbye that night." He admits. "I already knew I was leaving but I had to have a taste of you before I left. That taste has kept me going for the last five years, it was so fucking sweet! I should never have stopped, should have buried myself in you that night!"

That mental image is doing insane things to my mind and body, creating a pool of heated desire through my lower belly and a sudden moistness between my thighs.

"Why didn't you?" I whisper. "I would have let you."

"And now?" Tyler's eyes bore into mine and I can barely breathe from the intensity of that look.

I'm a goner and I don't care anymore if he knows it. "And now," I whisper.

TYLER

I break speed records as we head for my hotel. When she uttered those two words every fucking dream I've ever had came true.

There's no way I'm taking her home - the last thing we need right now is to be anywhere near anything that reminds us of our fathers'. But I'll be damned if our first time together is going to be some rushed affair on the back of a motorbike, and although the idea of sinking into her soft body on the Harley has my cock harder than a steel pole, I file that little fantasy away for another time. Right now, I want her naked on soft sheets in the middle of my bed where I can fuck her senseless in every way that I've imagined for the last five years.

The feel of her soft body behind me is torture. I can feel every soft curve pressed against me, her tits against my back, her thighs squeezing my hips, and it takes all my concentration not to crash the damn bike.

It doesn't take long to get to the hotel and I head straight into the underground garage, securing the bike in my parking spot.

I remove my helmet and turn to find that Jenna has already removed hers. She's still wearing my jacket, her cheeks flushed, her hair tangling around her shoulders and she's never looked more beautiful. Our gazes tangle as I reach for her hand and lead her to the elevator which will take us up to the lobby of the hotel.

I'm on her as soon as the doors close, backing her up against the elevator wall as my mouth crashes against hers. Grabbing her thighs, I lift her and pin her between me and the wall and she wraps her legs around my hips. I squeeze her rounded ass making her moan as she pushes her hips against mine, grinding her pussy against my throbbing cock.

The ping of the elevator reminds me where we are and I lower her back to her feet. We're breathing heavily and trying to compose ourselves as the doors open.

We cross the hotel lobby and take another elevator up to the tenth floor. Other guests file into in the cramped space so I have to keep my hands to myself until I have her in my room.

"Are you sure about this?" I ask her as I close the door behind us, hoping like hell that she's not about to change her mind.

She slips my jacket from her shoulders and pulls her t-shirt over her head. It drops to the floor next to my jacket and she stands there, her perfect tits cupped in a lacy little bra. I can see her hard nipples through the thin material and my cock swells to monumental proportions.

"I'll take that as a yes," I'm already moving towards her.

My mouth is on hers, our tongues tangling as I back her up until her knees hit the end of the bed. She falls backward onto the mattress, her hair splayed around her. She's every fucking fantasy I've ever had, right there in my bed and the sight of her nearly brings me to my knees.

I slide my hands up the outside of her thighs and across her waist, unbuttoning her jeans and peeling them down her legs. Starting at her ankle, I lick and nibble my way up the inside of her leg, almost reaching her moist center, before lavishing the same torturous treatment on the other leg.

"Ty, please!" she moans.

"Anything you want, baby," I say, "anything at all."

I unhook her bra, tossing it aside and bend to suckle one nipple, pinching the other between my thumb and finger.

Jenna arches up off the bed and her moans almost have me spilling my load right then and there.

I lick and kiss my way down her belly until I reach her soft pussy, loving her sweet scent as it surrounds me. The damp patch on her panties tells me just how turned on she is as I slip them down her legs, gently pressing her legs apart and opening her up to my lips. My tongue slides between her folds, finding her clit and giving it a firm lick which lifts her off the bed, choking out my name.

Fuck, I love hearing my name on her lips like that. It's taking everything I have not to strip off my clothes and plunge inside her, but I want to give her as much pleasure as I can first. My cock will have to wait a bit longer.

I continue to use my tongue on her as I feel the spasms that start to grip her body. I swirl and plunge my tongue against her nub and she cries out as her orgasm suddenly hits her, arching her off the bed and releasing her sweet juices into my mouth.

I keep up the pressure of my tongue a little longer, allowing her to milk her orgasm, the sounds she's making causing my cock to leak a little cum.

I stand, quickly stripping off my clothes and Jenna's eyes widen as she takes in the full, engorged length of me.

"Wow!" she breathes, and my cock swells even more under her rapt attention.

I kneel on the bed and pull her up in front of me, dipping my head to her mouth, the juices from her orgasm still coating my tongue. Her hands feather down my stomach before landing on my swollen cock.

"Holy fuck!" I groan, stilling her hands.

"Am I doing it wrong?" she asks uncertainly.

"No, baby. There's nothing that you could do wrong," I reassure her. "But, I'm right on the edge here, and if you carry on touching me like that I'm gonna shoot my load all over you.

"Oh."

Wrapping one arm around her waist I tip her backward so that she's under me and settle my weight on top of her. My dick slides between her still slick thighs and the friction is so exquisite I know I'm not going to be able to last much longer. I reach down and squeeze the base of my cock in an attempt to delay the inevitable.

"Are you on the pill?" I ask.

She shakes her head. "Never had any reason to be."

Shit! Is she saying what I think she is? "Why?" I ask, holding my breath.

"Because I've never been with anyone like this except for you," she says simply and a blush stains the skin from her magnificent tits up to her beautiful face.

My inner caveman is roaring and beating his chest as I gaze down at her. "Not in five years?"

"Not in the last five years or the next sixty-five," she says. "Not with anyone else. It's always been you for me since I was ten years old."

I close my eyes to hide their sudden sheen. This woman is going to be the death of me because I'm going to make love to her until my body gives out or I pop an artery!

I smooth her hair back from her flushed face and kiss her softly, reverently, teasing my tongue across her lips so that she opens up for me. It starts out gently but quickly becomes wild when she draws my lower lip into her mouth, sucking it gently.

"Where did you learn that?" I ask as a tiny spark of jealousy flickers to life in my chest.

"Just now, on you," she replies and the spark is doused as quickly as it ignited. "Did you like it?" she asks.

"Oh, I like it!" I growl. "I like everything you do to me."

"Really?" she waggles her eyebrows mischievously as she runs her hands down my back, opening her legs and wrapping them around my waist so that I'm pressed against her opening. My cock instantly wants to submerge itself in her and I can't fucking resist the urge anymore.

I reach into the bedside cabinet, pulling out a condom and tearing it open with my teeth before sheathing myself and settling back between her thighs.

"One day, I'll have you bareback," I promise, "with nothing between us." She obviously likes that thought as she moans and moves under me. I nuzzle her neck, moving down to her tits and flicking and sucking her nipples. "You taste and feel as amazing as I knew you would," I say as I dip my hand down and rub her clit with my thumb.

"Ty!" she moans my name and I increase the pressure and friction causing her hands to grab fistfuls of the sheets as she moves her hips instinctively. I press the tip of my cock to the entrance of her tight, hot pussy and slide in just a little way. She's so tight and I wonder if she'll be able to take all of my length. Who am I kidding? I've wanted her for so fucking long I'll only need one pump with my dick half-way in to shoot my load. She tenses and jerks underneath me as I push in a little further and I feel her hymen. Shit! It's thick and I know that this is going to be uncomfortable for her.

"I'm sorry baby, this is gonna hurt for a minute, but then I'll make it up to you, okay?"

"I don't care," she moans, "I just want you inside me, Ty! I've waited so long…..I love you!"

Her words splinter the last of my control and with one swift thrust, I bury myself in her warm tightness, clenching my teeth and forcing myself to stay still as her eyes close and she lets out a soft whimper.

I kiss her eyes, her cheeks, her mouth, trying to soothe her and after a minute I feel her muscles relax and her body open up even further to accept me.

She opens her eyes and looks at me "It's ok now."

It's all the encouragement I need. I move my hips slowly, letting her adjust to the size of my cock as I slide in and out of her wetness until I'm buried so deep that I don't know where I end and she begins. A grasp her hips and adjust her so that her I hit her clit with just the right friction each time I pump in and out, and the pressure begins to build behind my dick.

Electric shocks shoot up and down my spine as Jenna begins to climax beneath me. It's the most amazing fucking sight, seeing her throw her head back as she cries out. I feel the contractions deep inside her as she cums and knowing that I've given her that pleasure, that I'm her first, is enough to send me over the edge.

I roar as I succumb to my own orgasm, my release so intense that I think I may pass out. I rivet my hips to hers, my cock deep inside her as the last tendrils of pleasure slowly ebb away.

Breathing heavily, I collapse on top of her, careful not to crush her before rolling us onto our sides, our bodies still joined. I'm not ready to give up that connection just yet.

I wake with a start, breathing heavily in the grip of my nightmare, my body bathed in sweat, the smell of whiskey almost choking me.

Soft hands reach for me, soothing me and the terror fades a little with her touch. I remember where I am and who those soft hands belong to as she pulls me to her, wrapping herself around me as if she's trying to absorb my pain. For the first time ever following my nightmare, I'm able to succumb to sleep again.

JENNA

I open my eyes and it takes me a minute to remember where I am. When I do, a blush moves up my body from the tips of my toes and lands in my cheeks.

I stretch my arms above my head, feeling a soreness in places and muscles that have never been used before.

"Now, there's a sight to wake up to," a voice growls next to my ear.

I turn my head on the pillow to find Tyler propped on an arm facing me, his eyes on my exposed breasts where the sheet has slipped. "Good morning." I'm feeling a little shy and trying not to show it.

"It is!" Tyler replies, before reaching for me. He kisses me softly, lulling me into a false sense of security before suddenly standing and lifting me from the bed, throwing me over his shoulder in a firefighters lift.

"What are you doing?" I shriek, unable suppress the giggle that bubbles up from my throat.

"You're very dirty," Tyler replies matter-of-factly, "and I need to give you a thorough clean." He gives my bare butt a playful slap as he heads for the bathroom, turning on the shower and guiding me under the spray with him.

"You make me sound like a car," I laugh.

He waggles his eyebrows at me. "Let's see what's under the hood."

My laughter dies as he kneels in front of me, lathering the soap between his hands. He begins at my feet, working his way up my calves and knees until he reaches my thighs. His breath catches and he pauses, staring at me there and making me nervous.

"What's wrong?" I ask.

He slides a finger between my thighs and it comes away with a smear of blood. "Nothing," he replies. "Everything is fucking perfect. Last night was fucking perfect."

I blush as his meaning sinks in. "Don't get me wrong," he continues, "I wouldn't have cared if you'd been with a hundred men in the last five years," he pauses, "Christ, who the fucking hell am I trying to kid? I feel like strutting around like a stud with my chest out after last night - it made reading every one of those sex books worth it!"

"You read sex books?" I ask disbelievingly.

"Yeah. Loads of the fucking things. How else do you think I knew how to do those things I did to you last night?"

"Um….well….by practicing with….other women." The thought is like a knife in my belly.

He puts a finger under my chin and tilts it up so that so that we're looking directly at each other. "There haven't been any other women, Jen. Only you. Last night."

I'm shocked and search his eyes, seeing the truth of his words. "Wow! Those must have been some really good books! I think *I* need to read them."

He chuckles and the sound is wonderful, making me realize how long it is since I've heard his laugh. "Believe me, baby, you don't need any books to help get me off. All I need for that is your delectable body and your sweet pussy!"

I smack his arm, blushing. "We really need to work on that foul mouth."

"You love my foul mouth," he says. "You love it here," he feathers kisses across my eyes, "and here," he nuzzles my neck, "and especially here," he bends to suckle my breast, pulling the nipple into his mouth and grazing it with his teeth.

He's right, I do love his foul mouth.

He turns me so that my back is against his chest and I can feel his erection nudging against the crease at the top of my butt. He pumps some shampoo from the dispenser on the wall into his palm and works it into my hair, massaging my scalp. His hands feel like bliss as he rinses the suds away and repeats the process with the conditioner.

When he's done with my hair he transfers his attention to back to my body, his hands sliding over my slick skin, gently cupping my breasts as his thumbs flick over my nipples. They're still sensitive from his ministrations last night and my response is immediate, my head falling back against his shoulder as I moan my approval.

He growls in response and his hand dips down between my thighs, his fingers deft and sure as he opens me up to give him better access to work his magic. I can feel the heat building there like last night, but there's something I want more at the moment.

I turn in his arms and reach around him, squeezing some of the shampoo into my own hands, "My turn."

I start at his shoulders, lathering the shampoo down across his chest, grazing his nipples lightly with my fingers and following the ridges of his stomach muscles until I have his stiff shaft between both of my hands.

Tyler throws his head back with a grunt and I feel a surge of power as I tease him. His hands join mine, teaching, showing me the pressure and rhythm that he needs.

"Jen, I'm gonna cum if you keep that up," he moans, bending to claim my mouth with his.

"Then cum for me," I whisper against his lips and it's enough, his hips thrusting into my hands, his fingers tangling in my hair as the spasms rack his body and he unloads his seed between our bodies and into the water pooling at our feet.

My hands move up to spear through his hair as I kiss him gently while his breathing steadies. "I love kissing you," I whisper against his mouth, my tongue flicking across his lips. "I don't think I'll ever get tired of it."

He pulls me to him, wrapping me up in a bone crushing hug, his body shaking against mine in the aftermath of his release.

"Can't breathe!" I laugh, and he loosens his hold immediately, reaching to turn off the shower.

He grabs a couple of the fluffy hotel towels and proceeds to dry me before drying off himself, securing the towel low on his hips. Feeling a little exposed, I wrap myself in my own towel, tucking in the ends between my breasts.

Tyler reaches for my hand, sliding his fingers through mine and leads us from the bathroom. As we reach the bed I notice a small patch of blood on the sheets.

"I'm gonna get that framed," Tyler says, stripping the soiled sheet from the bed.

"Um….that would be a no," I reply, watching as he uses the top sheet to remake the bed, plumping the pillows and straightening the duvet which has ended up in a heap at the bottom of the bed sometime during the night. "Very domesticated," I tease.

"I aim to please," He grins. "Talking of which," he drops his towel and sits on the end of the freshly made bed, "now it's my turn." He opens his legs, beckoning me towards him and my stomach does a little flip-flop as I see that he's already more than capable again.

I move to stand in front of him and he reaches up to tug on the towel until it drops at my feet. He pulls me towards him, his mouth on a level with my stomach and my hands tangle in his hair and his mouth opens over the sensitive skin. His tongue delves into my navel before nibbling and licking his way across to one hip and then the other.

"Is that something you learned in one of those books?" I gasp, feeling the now familiar moistness between my thighs.

"Nope," he mumbles against my skin, "making this up as I go along,"

He tugs me off balance so that I'm straddling his lap, the end of his swollen shaft temptingly close to my opening. If I move just a few inches………

His hands still my hips. "Not yet. We have plenty of time. I want you screaming for me to fill you up!"

I moan at the imagery and he kisses me softly, his tongue flicking around the outside of my mouth as he bites and teases, pulling away so that my mouth follows his blindly, seeking a deeper contact.

"Please!" I'm not aware that I've even voiced the plea until his mouth crashes against mine, giving me what I want, my mouth opening as he sucks my tongue.

Sliding his hands under my thighs, he stands, lifting me with him as I wrap my arms around his neck. He turns towards the bed, following me down as he lowers me gently to the mattress. His hand smooths down between my thighs and he slips a finger inside me, followed by another, stretching me open while he uses his thumb against the most sensitive part of me. The feel of his fingers and thumb teasing and stroking has me hotter than a furnace as I press myself against his hand, wanting more.

"Tyler!" I gasp. "I need you inside me. Please!" I want…..*need* all of him, need to feel him buried in me, as close as we were last night.

He pulls his fingers from me, licking them clean and whilst I'm sure the memory will embarrass me later, right now it's one of the hottest things I've ever seen. But he's not done tormenting me yet, his head dipping to my breasts, pulling and sucking at my nipples until I'm in a frenzy, wrapping my legs around his hips and trying to bring him to me, into me.

"Tyler!" I moan his name again, a note of desperation in my voice.

He reaches for a condom, quickly sliding it down himself and I vaguely think that I'm going to take great pleasure in doing that for him one of these days.

"Okay, baby." He moves his hips down so that I can feel the end of him against me and pauses. He looks down at me, holding my gaze. "You're mine!" he growls. "Say it!"

"I'm yours, Tyler," I pant.

He enters me with one smooth thrust of his hips and I cry out at the fullness of him, my body stretching to accommodate his length and width. He reaches between our joined bodies and his thumb finds my hard, little nub, sweeping back and forth until I come undone beneath him.

I sob his name as the pleasure hits me, intensified by the pounding of his body into mine, barely aware of his shout as he finds his own release and his weight settles on top of me.

I hold him to me, our foreheads pressed together, my legs still wrapped around his hips and our bodies still joined as I stroke my hands up and down his back. Slowly our breathing returns to normal and we sleep.

I wake up some time later to the delicious smell of coffee and pastries being wafted under my nose. "Mmmmmn, is that coffee I smell?" I open my eyes to find Tyler placing a mug of coffee and a croissant on the bedside cabinet before he sits on the edge of the bed next to me.

I pull myself into a sitting position. My stomach gives a loud gurgle and I realize that I haven't eaten since lunchtime yesterday. "Gimme! I need caffeine!" I take a sip of the steaming coffee, before taking a huge bite from the buttery croissant, sighing as the combination hits my taste-buds. "Are you not eating?" I mumble through another mouthful.

Tyler leans forward to claim a kiss, lingering to lick a few flakes of pastry from my mouth. "I'll eat when I get back."

"When you get back? Where are you going?"

"Just for a run," he replies. "I need to blow off some steam." Despite being a big guy, there's not an ounce of fat on him, a fact I now know intimately.

"After last night? And this morning?" I waggle my eyebrows at him.

"Different kind of steam," he chuckles. "Running is good thinking time. I won't be long." He gives me a quick kiss.

After he leaves, I head for the bathroom, cleaning my teeth using the little complimentary pack of toothpaste and toothbrush before taking a quick shower. I dry off, smiling to myself, as I pluck my clothes from various parts of the floor.

I'm finger combing my hair when I hear a vibrating sound coming from the bedside drawer. Opening it, I flush as I see the box of condoms next to the cell phone which is lit up with the caller ID 'Jake'.

Before I can think, I grab it. "Hello?"

"Well, hello!" says a deep rumble. "I'm guessing that's not you Ty," the voice continues, "unless you're wearing your particularly tight pants."

I laugh. "No tight pants here, I'm afraid!"

"In that case, you must be Jenna."

"How do you know my name?" I ask.

"Ty told me he was coming back for the funeral, so I'm guessing it was your Mom?" There's a pause before he adds, "I'm sorry for your loss."

"Thank you," I reply, something about his genuine tone causing a prickle of tears behind my eyes. I clear my throat. "Ty's not here right now. Can I get him to call you?"

"Nah, that's ok thanks. It's nothing important. I'll call him again later. Nice talking to you, Jenna."

"You too, Jake."

As I replace the phone I notice an envelope pushed to the back of the drawer. The insignia on the top right corner catches my eye. I hesitate, a strange sense of foreboding washing over me as I pluck the envelope from the drawer and pull out the contents of the unsealed envelope.

My stomach sinks to my feet and I can feel the blood draining from my face as I realize what I'm holding. A contract. Signed at the bottom by Tyler McCade.

It seems that Tyler never had any intentions of staying here. I know my football insignias, having grown up with a father who's made his living from the game, and this one is on the west coast. So, that's where he's ended up.

Almost 2000 miles away.

On the opposite side of the country.

And it was all decided before he even got here.

I tuck the papers back into the drawer, my fingers numb as tears leak from the corners of my eyes.

Tyler has been my fantasy for as long as I can remember, but the reality of being with him has far exceeded my expectations. I don't feel like I'll ever be able to get enough of him and that scares me senseless because, once again, it seems he doesn't feel the same, not if this contract is anything to go by.

I think back over our time together since he returned and realize that he's never made any suggestion of a permanent commitment outside of a sexual nature. Telling me that I'm 'his' is hardly a declaration of love. I'm not so naive that I don't know the promises people make to each other during the act of sex.

I know the abuse he suffered at the hands of his father made him feel unworthy and wary of a relationship - it's a big part of the reason he left in the first place.

He confessed this morning that I was his first, just as he was mine. Surely, that has to mean something, doesn't it? Or has he just come back to bury old demons and put the past behind him once and for all before returning to his own life? Without me.

I quickly dash away my tears as I hear the door open and Tyler enters, looking hot, sweaty and utterly gorgeous. I summon up the best fake smile I can muster as I look at him, but he's not fooled and frowns as he strides towards me.

"What's up?" His blue eyes are dark with worry as he sees the tear stains on my cheeks. "What's happened?"

"Nothing." I shake my head as fresh tears flow. I'm not ready to confess what I found in the drawer or to share my insecurities with him. I need some time to process. "It's just the last few weeks catching up with me since Mom died, and then the funeral, and you, and all the stuff with Dad…….." I'm babbling and clamp by mouth shut.

Tyler cups my face and uses his thumbs to wipe away my tears. "No. *I'm* sorry." He pulls me into his arms, stroking my hair. "I've been so caught up in the past since I've been back I've forgotten that you're still in mourning for your Mom. I know my timing is crappy but I came back to put things right so that we can both move on with our lives, have some closure."

My heart cracks a little and I wonder if he knows what he's just confessed. He wants us to move on with our lives. Separately. He just needed to put things straight first. "It's okay," I school my expression while my heart lies in two pieces in my chest. "I'm sorry for blubbing all over you." I give him an Oscar worthy smile. "Now, go grab a shower before you catch your death," It obviously convinces him this time because he turns and heads to the bathroom.

He closes the door and as soon as I hear the shower spray, I grab my purse and keys, trying not to remember as I step over his leather jacket still lying in the middle of the floor and quietly close the door behind me.

This time, I need to be in control of my fate. This time, I'm walking away from him before he walks away from me.

TYLER

I take my time in the shower, washing away the sweat from my run and remembering how fucking beautiful it was, standing here and shooting my load into Jenna's soft hands. Just the thought has me ready for action again. I swear I'll never be able to get enough of that woman. I'm a walking hard-on where she's concerned.

It's hard to believe that I've been back for less than two days and how much has happened in that time. I came back here with a pipe dream and ended up with a fucking wet dream to end all wet dreams in the shape of dark brown eyes and a body made for sin - but only with me. Only ever with me. The solace I find in her beautiful smile and delectable body has given me a kind of peace that I've never known before.

And when she said she loved me I thought I'd fucking died and gone to Heaven. If she can love a man like me, with all my scars, then maybe I'm not as damaged as I thought. I can still have the normal life I've always wanted.....with her.

Because I love her too. And not the pretty hearts and roses kind of love, but the gut-wrenching, do-anything-for-her kind of love. If love is a disease, I've got it and it's getting worse. And I wouldn't have it any other way.

I turn off the shower, realizing I've spent far longer than I meant to daydreaming about Jenna. Shit! That woman has me wound so tight around her little finger I'd walk naked over hot coals with lead weights tied to my balls so long as she was waiting on the other side.

Still drying myself, I wander back into the bedroom to find it empty. Jenna's coffee cup still sits on the bedside cabinet from earlier, but there's no sign of her. Maybe she went to grab some fresh air. As I'm pondering on that my cell phone begins to vibrate.

I pluck it from the bedside drawer. "Hey, Jake."

"Ah, it's you this time!" Jake's voice booms down the line.

"Who else would it be, you dick?"

"Now, now! Don't be calling your best friend names like that. Nobody likes a potty mouth." Jake pretends to be offended although I've called him far worse in the past. "I thought perhaps it might be the lovely Jenna again."

"Jenna?"

"Yeah. I called earlier but you were out. Anything you wanna share?"

"Not a fucking chance."

"Okay. I see how it is. Listen," Jake's voice takes on a more serious note, "I know you've got shit to sort out there, but Coach Cole is chafing my ass about where the fuck you are and when the fuck you'll be back - his words, not mine."

"I need a few more days, Jake. Can you stall him a bit longer for me?" I ask.

Jake sighs. "Yeah, sure man - but you owe me a tube of Lanacane for my chafed ass!"

That's a mental image I won't be able to forget anytime soon. "I'll buy you a crate," I chuckle. "And thanks."

"Yeah, yeah. I'm nothin' if not your bitch! And Ty? All joking aside - make the decision for you, not for anyone else."

"Yeah. Been there, done that, got the hashtag." I reply.

I hang up and as I toss the phone back, my eyes fall to the envelope in the drawer. Things start clicking over in my head - and not in a good way.

Jenna answered my phone earlier and spoke to Jake.

She saw the letter.

And she's not here.

"Fuck!" I dress in a frenzy, scooping my jacket off the floor and grabbing my keys before heading out the door.

JENNA

I've been home half an hour when the banging starts at the front door. I really wasn't sure if he would follow me back or if he'd be relieved to find me gone so that he could leave without a scene. Demons slayed, no recriminations.

"Jenna!" Another thump rattles the door in its frame. "I know you're in there, Jenna!"

I march to the front door and swing it open, halting his hand mid-thump. "Come in, Tyler." I turn and walk towards the kitchen, leaving him to follow.

I fill the kettle to keep my hands busy and to hide their slight tremor. "Coffee?" I ask Tyler, even though I've never known him to drink a cup of the stuff in his life.

"What the fuck, Jenna?" Tyler explodes, ignoring my question. "Why did you take off like that?"

I turn to face him, leaning back against the counter, my heart beating out of my chest. "Your cell rang and I answered it. It was in the bedside drawer. I saw the contract." Some the fire goes out of his eyes and I can see that I've just confirmed a suspicion he'd already had. "When Dad told me he'd gotten you a full-ride scholarship, I didn't know quite how far it was." I pause. "Or where it would take you professionally. Congratulations. You're about to become the new linebacker for one of the biggest teams in the country."

"Jenna…."

"Why did you really come back, Ty?" I interrupt him. "To slay old dragons? Put the past to rest and tie up loose ends? Am I a loose end? God, what an idealistic idiot I am!" I choke the words through a throat thick with emotion.

"Jenna…." Ty tries again, but this time the jangle of house phone interrupts us, making us both jump.

I turn numbly and pluck the receiver from the cradle mounted on the kitchen wall. "Hello?"

"Ms. Danvers?" I'm not familiar with the female voice on the end of the line. "Yes, this is Jenna Danvers." A feeling of unease unfurls in my stomach.

"Ms. Danvers, this is Mary Jacobs from Ruby Memorial Hospital in West Virginia. We've been trying to contact you since last night. We have a Mr. Michael Danvers here - your father I believe. He's been in an accident."

TYLER

Jenna's eyes widen in horror and her hand flies to her mouth and I know something is seriously wrong. I can tell she's gone into shock, so I gently take the phone from her nerveless fingers, holding it up to my ear.

It only takes a few minutes to get the information I need and I replace the phone. I turn and reach for Jenna and she allows me to pull her into my arms, probably due more to shock than any desire to be held by me at the moment. "Go and pack an overnight bag, baby." She just looks at me. "The hospital is five hours away." I explain gently. She nods woodenly and heads towards her bedroom.

Her father was driving upstate into West Virginia when his car had been tail-gated by a truck that had run a red light. He'd suffered multiple injuries but, thank God, none of them are life-threatening. Not that Jenna seems to comprehend that right now. Shit! She must be torn up inside. First her Mom, and now this! She and I have things we need to sort out, but they'll have to wait. Right now the priority is to get her to her Dad.

Jenna comes back into the kitchen, holding a small rucksack, her face pale.

"We'll take the bike. It'll be quicker." I say.

Jenna shakes her head. "No, I'll drive. There's no need for you to come."

I am so not having this fucking argument. "You're not going on your own even if I have to throw you over my shoulder and tie you to the bike!" The thought of tying Jenna to the Harley raises some inappropriate thoughts that are *really* not suitable right now. "It'll be quicker on the bike than taking your car." She can't argue with my logic there and gives a little nod of her head as a sign that she agrees, even though I can see that it's against her better judgment.

Jenna grabs a jacket and shrugs the rucksack on her back as we leave the house. I climb on and start the bike while Jenna situates herself stiffly behind me, a far cry from the woman who molded her every curve to my back last night.

We make a quick detour to the hotel so that I can grab my a few things for myself and we're back on the road and heading up the I-79.

The light is fading as we reach the hospital almost five hours later, having only stopped briefly for gas and to use the bathroom.

I park the Harley and we head straight to the hospital reception.

"Hi. I'm Jenna Danvers. I understand my father was admitted here last night? Michael Danvers?"

The receptionist, a middle-aged woman with blonde hair, taps away on the computer, checking patient admissions until she finds what she's looking for. "Ah, here you go, honey. He's been moved to Room 242. Just follow the signs to the left there to take the elevator up to the second floor."

Once in the elevator I hit the button for the second floor. Despite having spent the last five hours on a bike together, Jenna has thrown up a physical and emotional wall between us and it's pissing me off. The last time we were in an elevator I'd pinned her up against the wall in a frenzy of need but the closeness that we shared last night and this morning seems to have been erased with one misunderstanding. A misunderstanding I aim to put right once this is all over. But right now, making sure her father is okay is the main priority.

I slow as we approach the door to her father's room and Jenna turns to look at me with a question in her eyes.

"I'll go grab us a drink while you go on in." She looks relieved. I know she needs this time alone with her father. "I'll be close by if you need me." Unexpectedly, she reaches out for my hand, grasping it for a second as she says, "Thank you, Tyler." She looks so vulnerable in that moment that it's all I can do not to wrap her up in my arms and try to take away her pain like she did for me last night.

Instead, I just nod and head off down the hall.

JENNA

There's a dim light illuminating the room as I step inside and it takes a few seconds for my eyes to adjust.

When they do, my hands fly to my mouth at the sight of my Dad. He's hooked up to a blood pressure monitor and an IV line stands at his bedside, directing fluids and pain meds into his body via the back of his hand. His face is bruised, a dressing covering what looks to be a nasty cut over his left eye and a cast covers his right leg from just above his toes to mid thigh.

Although it doesn't seem like it right now, he's been lucky. The thought of what could have happened makes my stomach turn over, especially after the way things were between us when he left.

Dad stirs in the bed, groaning a little before his eyes focus on me. "Jenna?"

"Dad!" I'm at his side in an instant, reaching for his hand as tears spill down my cheeks. "God, you scared me! I thought I'd lost you too!"

"Hey, hey," Dad says huskily, reaching up to stroke my hair, "I'm not going anywhere, kid. It'll take more than a semi to take me out," he jokes, then coughs, holding his bruised ribs.

"I'm so sorry I wasn't here sooner. I didn't get the call from the hospital until this afternoon. They'd been trying to contact me since last night, but I was out with…." I stumble to a halt.

"Tyler. You were out with Tyler," Dad finishes for me. "It's okay, Jenna. You don't have to be worried about saying his name in front of me." Dad grimaces, shifting his position slightly to get more comfortable. "I know I messed up. I should never have interfered back then. Everything you said to me the other night was true. I did judge Tyler. I judged him based on the word of an abusive drunk and I'll never forgive myself for not seeing through his lies. For someone who prides himself on his instincts when it comes to work, I really did drop the ball when it comes to Tyler - no pun intended." Dad smiles weakly at his own joke. "I was away so much when you were growing up that I think I overcompensated when I was home. Anyone who wanted to be with my little girl had impossibly high standards to live up to and I thought Tyler didn't come close. I couldn't have been more wrong." He rests his head back against the pillows behind him, closing his eyes.

"We don't need to talk about this now, Dad," I say, concerned.

"Yes. We do." Dad replies firmly, lifting his head and fixing me with the dark brown eyes that look so much like my own. "If being here has taught me anything," he gestures at the hospital room around him, "it's that you can't leave things unsaid."

He pauses before continuing, "Before you told me the truth of Tyler's circumstances, I told you that it didn't take much convincing to get Tyler to leave. That's not strictly true. He told me that the *only* reason he would take me up on my offer was because he thought it was the best thing for you." Dad sees my confused look. "Tyler left because he wanted to make something of his life. So that he could come back to you when he felt he had something to offer you."

"But he always had something to offer me!" I protest. "Himself! He just never thought he was enough."

"I know," Dad says sadly. "And I played a big part in that - something that I'll spend the rest of my days trying to make up for. I thought you were too young to fall in love, but I was wrong there too. I, of all people, should have known better, because I fell in love with your mother the first time I ever laid eyes on her when I was sixteen." Dad's eyes glisten with unshed tears. "I've made so many mistakes as a father. I'm sorry. I'm so, so sorry!"

I reach out to him and we're crying and hugging each other as best as we can around tubes and wires, careful not to jostle his injuries.

"It's okay, Dad, It's okay," I soothe, as if I'm the parent consoling the child. "It doesn't matter now anyway." I take two tissues from the the box on the bedside cabinet and hand one to Dad, keeping the other to wipe my own eyes.

"What do you mean, it doesn't matter?" Dad asks.

"Tyler's leaving," I reply.

"Leaving where?"

"California. He's been signed. I saw the contract. It's a done deal. He may have come back, but it was only to tie up loose ends, put the past to rest. It wasn't for me." I feel tears threatening again.

"I don't believe that," Dad says, shaking his head. "You need to talk to him. Ask him. I saw the way he looked at you at the cemetery - it was the same way he looked at you all those years ago. If you really love him you need to fight for him." Dad can't know that he's repeating almost the exact same words I said to Tyler last night. I accused Tyler of not fighting for me. Am I brave enough to fight for him?

I sigh, feeling closer to my dad in this moment than at any other time in my life. "Thanks, Dad. I'll talk to him."

"Good girl," Dad pats my hand. "Now, I assume Tyler didn't let you come alone and is hiding around here somewhere?" I nod, smiling inside at the idea that Tyler would hide from my Dad. "Well, go find him and let your old man get some sleep."

"Are you sure? I don't want to leave you." I protest.

"I'm sure. Go. And get some rest yourself."

"Okay. I'll be back first thing." I kiss my Dad on the cheek and head towards the door, pausing with my hand on the door handle, "Dad?" Dad looks at me. "I love you."

Dad clears his throat before answering, "I love you too, kid."

TYLER

I'm sitting in a chair down the hall when Jenna comes out of the room. I can see she's been crying and the need to take her in my arms almost overwhelms me again. I stuff my hands in the pockets of my jeans instead. "How is he?"

"Tired and bruised but better than I was expecting." Jenna replies, stifling a yawn.

"Come on. You're dead on your feet. I've booked us a hotel about ten minutes from here. Don't panic - separate rooms." I say, lying through my ass. No way are we staying in separate rooms tonight – not happening.

We leave the hospital and less than ten minutes later we're at the hotel. It's not hard to convince Jenna to sit in one of the hotel lobby chairs while I check us in, tired as she is.

I slip key card into the lock, holding the door open so that Jenna can walk in ahead of me. I follow her in, shut and lock the door behind me and walk towards her, shrugging off my jacket and removing my t-shirt on the way.

"Tyler," she says nervously, lifting her hands to my chest as if to ward me off. I moan as her hands make contact with my bare skin. She's got me so fucking tied up in knots that one touch is almost enough to make me cum in my jeans.

Before she has chance to say anything else, I bend to her mouth and kiss her, a gentle, teasing touch of my mouth against hers until she's the one moaning and seeking a deeper contact, which I'm more than happy to provide as I sweep my tongue into her mouth.

"Do you have any fucking idea what you do to me?" I ask, lifting my mouth from hers an inch.

She looks deep into my eyes. "You mean physically?"

"Definitely physically." Her eyes drop. I tip her chin up so that she's looking at me again. "But mostly emotionally. Mentally. Spiritually. When I'm with you I feel like I'm home."

Her breath catches as she looks at me, searching my eyes for something. "But…...the contract?"

"Fuck the contract!"

Her eyes widen at my outburst. "But, you signed it!"

"Yeah, I signed it. I signed it before I came back here. Before I knew there was any possibility of a 'you and me'. Didn't it occur to you that I haven't mailed it? Jake has been stalling for me for weeks, buying me some time." Her eyes widen with understanding.

"When I heard about Maggie, I couldn't stay away any longer. I'm only sorry that it took the loss of your Mom to give me the kick up the ass I needed, the courage to at least come and try. I knew I had to be here for you, even if you looked at me with disgust. Even if you still hated me for leaving."

Jenna places her palm against my cheek. "I told you last night, Ty. I've never hated you. I never could." I turn my face and kiss her palm.

"I stayed away for five years, Jenna. Five of the longest fucking years of my life! The longer I stayed away, the harder it was to come back. My father did a number on me, Jen, and I was sure that I'd never be good enough, whole enough. Just…....enough." I pause to catch my breath, long buried emotions spewing out of me like water from a geyser.

"One thing I've learned being back here is that I can't outrun my past. I don't want to anymore, because no matter how bad it was, no matter what that bastard did to me, my past also includes you. You were the light that kept me going, kept me breathing, kept me fighting. You still are." I bend to claim her mouth in a soft kiss. "It was never about the football", I whisper against her lips, "it was about you. And me. I ran away from you five years ago. This morning, you tried to run away from me, but no more. No more running. We'll work out the details, Jen, but from now on, I go where you go because that's where home is for me - with you." I kiss the tear that leaks from the corner of her eye.

"You love me!" she says, as if it's only just fucking dawning on her.

"Love you. Adore you. Wanna spend my life fucking your brains out and eating steak pies with you."

"At the same time?" she smiles that perfect smile, the one that burns me up inside every time I'm lucky enough to see it.

"Now there's a thought! Your sweet pussy *and* steak pie. My God, I'll die a happy man!" I groan.

Jenna slaps my bare chest. "Will you stop talking about my vagina like it's your own personal pet!" she laughs.

"But it is mine, baby. All mine. And I'm about to stroke it 'til it purrs."

She makes no protest as I swing her up in my arms and walk to the bed, letting her body slide down mine as I bend my head to hers and claim her mouth in a kiss.

Her hands reach up to tangle in my hair as my lips travel from her mouth to her ear, flicking the tender spot behind and biting the lobe before traveling down her neck. Jenna's head falls back and the vibration of her moan against my mouth turns my cock into a hungry, moisture-seeking missile. Fuck this! I need her. Right now. I need to be inside her, as close as I can get. And from the way she's grinding her pussy against me, she feels the same way.

Our clothes come off in a frenzy and we tumble onto the bed, not even bothering to strip the duvet down, so desperate are we for each other. I slide my hand down her body, over her soft stomach, and between her legs. She's already wet for me as I slide first one, then two fingers inside her tight cavity, swirling her clit with my thumb. She comes up off the bed with a hoarse moan as I thumb her, spreading her juices around her soft folds as I suck her nipples into tight pebbles.

I know I'm not gonna be able to last long but I don't think that's going to be a problem as Jenna is already arching off the bed as her orgasm slams into her body and I feel the contractions of her tight hole around my fingers. The sensation of her cumming is so fucking hot, making the need to submerge myself in her overwhelming.

I reach for my abandoned jeans, pulling a condom from the pocket and tearing the packet open. As I go to put it on, Jenna's hand covers mine.

"Let me," she says and plucks it from my hand. "Lie down," she instructs and Holy fuck, it's hot having her take control.

I lie on my back and Jenna straddles me, bending forwards so that she can kiss me, her tits rubbing against my chest. She grasps my cock and slowly, slowly sheaths my engorged length with the condom.

"I've been wanting to do that since this morning," she breathes against my mouth, biting my lower lip gently and making my cock jerk. She positions herself so that the end of my shaft is against her wet opening.......and stops. I try to push up into her but she backs off, lifting her hips away from mine. "No need to rush," she purrs, "we've got all night." It's official - my cock is gonna explode.

Jenna trails her hands down my chest, her fingers circling my nipples before dipping down my abs until she has my balls cupped in her soft palms. The touch is excruciating, amazing, fan-fucking-tastic as she explores me, finding sensitive spots even I didn't know I had.

"Jenna!" Her name is a growl.

"You're mine," she says, her warm, brown eyes full of so much love it takes my breath away. "Say it."

"I'm yours, Jen. Always." She's just used my own words to her this morning in the most satisfying way possible and I've got no pride where this woman of mine is concerned.

It's all she needs to hear and in one movement she sinks down on my cock, taking me to the hilt and making us both cry out. She stills for a few seconds, holding me deep, her muscles squeezing around the base of my shaft and the feeling of her tight warmth is indescribable. My hands fall to her hips, helping her find a rhythm and then my woman is riding me like a natural. Man, she's a fast learner. Her hips rise and fall in time with my thrusts, our bodies coming together with wets slaps as her juices bathe us, the sound all the more erotic as my orgasm begins to build. And then It's on me in a heated rush as I cum with one final thrust, a groan tearing itself from my throat at the exquisite release.

As I calm down, I hear Jenna still whimpering on top of me. I was a goner when she started riding me and I suddenly realize that I didn't last long enough for her to reach her own orgasm.

In one swift movement, I flip her onto her back, my cock still buried deep inside her. "Okay, baby. I'm gonna take care of you now." I bend to suckle her nipples, grazing my teeth over the tight buds. She's close and my mouth on her tits is all it takes before she's spasming in my arms and throbbing around my dick.

Our breathing slowly comes back to normal and although I don't want to separate my body from hers, I head to the bathroom to clean up. One day soon we're gonna to have each other with no barriers in between us.

I climb back into bed, pulling the covers over us as Jenna curls herself around me. We still have stuff to sort out – life isn't perfect but with Jenna next to me, it's pretty fucking close. For the first time in a long time, I fall into a dreamless sleep.

EPILOGUE
10 months later

JENNA

"TOUCHDOWN!"

The commentator's voice announces the win and the stadium erupts. Prue screams, jumping up and down next to me, her long, red hair swinging around her shoulders and her generous breasts moving independently to the rest of her voluptuous body. Prue is blissfully unaware of the male attention she draws as she bounces up and down in excitement. You'd never guess it was her first time at a game.

Prue is as bubbly, outspoken and full of life as I am quiet and reserved and she and I hit if off the moment we met when I moved here to California just over a month ago. I would never have believed ten months ago that I would be sitting here now, on the other side of the country.

It hadn't taken me long to decide that I would follow Tyler here, despite Tyler's protests that he would give up this amazing opportunity to stay with me. We both needed a fresh start, away from the memories of Tyler's abuse at the hands of his father and all that had followed. He wasn't running away this time, I'd reassured him, because you can't run away from yourself - something we'd both learned the hard way. He was facing the memories that had shackled him for so long and finally beginning to make his peace with them. It was a start.

The nine months we spent apart was torture, despite the days and nights we managed to snatch here and there wherever we could. I'd had to work my notice at the leisure complex and find a job here and in my absence, Tyler had found us a beautiful apartment in a quiet part of town. Luckily, my skills were transferable and I'd been hired as the Manager at a sports and remedial facility just outside of town. It's a little different than I'm used to but the principles of running it are similar and I'm enjoying the new challenge. It's how I met Prue, who is one of our best therapists and that kind of makes me her boss, although the thought of anyone bossing Prue around makes me chuckle. She's no wilting wallflower but she has a vulnerability that she hides well and a heart as big as anyone I've ever met.

I look back to the football pitch, my eyes immediately drawn like magnets to Tyler amongst the other players. I could pick that man out blindfolded in a line-up. Now there's a tempting thought, Tyler blindfolded and at my mercy. Food for thought.

"There's Tyler," I point him out to Prue. "And that's Jake, next to him." I have to admit to being a little intimidated the first time I met Jake – I thought Tyler was a big guy but Jake is a mountain of a man with a reputation for the ladies, according to Tyler.

Prue's sunny personality temporarily goes into eclipse as she fixes Jake with a glare, her eyes spitting fire at him. Seems like there might be a little history there, but I don't know Prue well enough yet to pry. She quickly wipes the expression from her face before turning to hug me. "That was amazing! Thank you so much for bringing me!"

I chuckle at her excitement, "Anytime. It makes a nice change to have someone to sit with. I'm not sure what was more entertaining, watching you or watching the game!"

"I know, I know! I did get a little over-excited but I couldn't help it. All those manly specimens at the peak of physical fitness with butt cheeks that could crack walnuts and enormous di....."

"Okay, okay!" I interrupt, holding my hands up, knowing where this conversation is headed. "It's good to know you came for the tactical strategies of the game," I laugh.

"Nah – I just came for the hot men in tight pants," Prue says shamelessly, fanning herself dramatically with her hands.

My cell rings just as we're collecting our belongings and heading out of the stands. I nod as Prue mouths that she'll meet me back at her car as I take the call.

"I knew they could do it!" Dad's voice booms at me down the line.

"Never doubted it Dad, never doubted it." I chuckle. "How are you?"

I haven't seen him since moving here, although we talk often on the phone. After his accident, he was transferred to a hospital closer to home before being discharged. His recovery is taking longer than his impatient nature would like, mostly down to the injury to his leg, which he's still having physio for.

"Ah, you know. Missing you. It's not the same without you - this place feels empty without you and your Mom." The pain of losing Mom is still there for both of us and I know that it'll never go away. I don't want it to because if I deny the pain and sorrow at losing her then I deny the special bond of love we shared. "I may even have to move closer to you and Tyler." The thought warms me. Our relationship has come a long way since Dad's accident. Nothing like a near-death experience to crystallize what's important.

"I miss you too, Dad. And I'd love that. We both would." Tyler and Dad's relationship is still a work in progress. Tyler's not one to hold a grudge but it's taken a while for him to trust that Dad won't interfere again despite how sorry Dad is for how he went about things. It's hard to deny though, that he did do Tyler a favor in the long run and a part of Tyler respects that Dad was only trying to look out for me, even if his motives were misplaced. They both love me, so there's common ground right there and hopefully, the rest will follow over time.

"Really?" Dad says, a rare thread of insecurity weaving through his voice.

"Really."

"Well then," Dad clears his throat, "I guess I'll start looking."

I say my goodbyes, promising to call him in a few days before heading back to the parking lot. As I approach, I'm surprised to hear Prue's voice raised in anger.

".......told you, you big, muscle-bound jackass, I was nowhere near your precious car!"

"And I told *you*, Carrots, if there's any damage, it'll be on your insurance!" A deep, familiar voice rumbles back. I peek around the corner to see Jake and Prue nose-to-nose in a stand-off; or rather, nose to nipple in Prue's case, being as she's a full head shorter than Jake.

"Don't. Call. Me. Carrots! My name is Prudence, not Anne Fucking Shirley!" Prue's complexion almost matches her hair and she's vibrating with anger. "Not that you'd remember," she adds enigmatically under her breath.

Jake looks confused for a second, the Anne of Green Gables reference obviously going straight over his head. "Well, whatever-the-fuck-your-name-is, look where you're going before reversing your car. You won't be so fortunate next time!" Jake forces the words out between clenched teeth before turning on his heel, climbing into his Ferrari and driving off with a squeal of tires.

"Stupid, overbearing, arrogant......"

"I see you've met Jake," I'm really trying to be a good friend and not laugh at Prue's mutterings.

"Oh, I've met him before," Prue replies, reminding me of her earlier comment as pain flashes briefly in her eyes. I raise my eyebrows in question. "Never mind," she mutters, climbing into the driver's seat of her VW Jetta. I wonder at Prue's closed expression, so at contrast with her usual sunny personality but decide not to pursue the subject. "Come on. Let's get you home so you can get into femme fatale mode before Tyler gets back." All sign of her previous bad mood is gone as she waggles her eyebrows suggestively at me.

Twenty minutes later I'm unlocking the door to the apartment, kicking off my shoes as I walk through to the kitchen. The whole apartment is open-plan, with a small entranceway leading to the kitchen, living and dining area. There are two bedrooms leading off a hallway from the dining area, both with en-suites. It even has a private garage attached to the side and accessed through a door off the kitchen where Tyler keeps the Harley. Tyler and I have added our own touches to the place, making it homely. Making it ours.

I head to the master bedroom, taking a quick shower and washing and drying my hair before slipping on the piece of clothing I've bought especially for this occasion.

I drape myself over the king-size bed, anticipation swirling in my stomach as I hear the throb of the Harley's engine out front.

Tyler's home.

TYLER

"Jenna?"

No answer. That's odd. She's usually waiting to launch herself into my arms and fuck me senseless after a win. "Jen, baby?" I head for the bedroom, throw open the door and come to a sudden halt, my mouth dropping open.

"Holy shit!"

Jenna is lying on her side on the bed wearing nothing but a leather jacket, the tiniest of black panties and a smile. The jacket is open down the front revealing the swell of her tits and finishes just at the tops of her thighs, giving me a tantalizing, cock-twitching view of her lace covered pussy.

"I thought it was about time I had my own jacket," she breathes, lifting one side away from her body slightly so that I get an eyeful of one of her perfect tits, it's nipple hard and begging for my mouth. "I can't keep borrowing yours. Well? Are you going to just stand there staring?" Jenna moves restlessly on the bed, her eyes burning into mine and promising me all kinds of sinful delights. Fuck me, I'll buy her ten fucking leather jackets if it means I get to come home to this every night!

I don't need any further prompting and slowly approach the bed, giving her a show of my own as I strip off my clothes one item at a time so that she's breathing heavily by the time I'm naked in front of her. My cock stands out proudly in front of me, ready to report for duty.

Unexpectedly I swoop down and pluck Jenna from the bed, ignoring her surprised squeal as I throw her over my shoulder, much as I did that first morning in the hotel room. Only this time, I'm not taking her to the shower.

"What are you doing?" She laughs as I head through the kitchen and fling open the access door to the garage.

"Something I've wanted to do for some time now," I reply. She shivers at the lower temperature in the garage, goose-bumps breaking out over exposed skin as I use my spare hand to tug her panties down, ripping them in the process and tossing them aside. She'll soon be warm, hot even.

I place her gently on the seat of the Harley, facing forwards as if she's driving and climb on behind her. I pull her back against me, pressing my swollen cock against her butt as I slip my hands around the front of her thighs, pulling them apart to give me access to her wet slit. She mewls as I find her clit with my fingers, her pussy clenching and grinding against my hand instinctively as I circle and stroke her hard little nub. "Oh, that feels so good!" she moans, tipping her head back against my shoulder.

Keeping one thumb against her clit, I move the other hand up to her luscious tit, rolling the hard nipple between my fingers and eliciting another moan of pleasure as I grind my swollen cock against her from behind.

Not satisfied, Jenna swivels on the seat to face me, her hands grasping my thick shaft as she dips her head and sips the clear fluid from the top, licking it like it's a fucking popsicle. My hands go to the back of her head and tangle in her hair as she dips her mouth up and down, taking as much of my length as she can, her tongue flicking and teasing around the sensitive end until I think my fucking balls are gonna explode.

Jenna lifts her head and repositions her body, wriggling so that her thighs are on top of mine, the end of my cock hovering at her slick pussy. She looks like every mans wet dream dressed only in the leather jacket - but she's mine. All mine.

"I want you inside me. Now."

I'm only too happy to fulfil her request and I impale her with one swift thrust, almost cumming immediately with the sheer pleasure of feeling her tight channel with nothing between us. There's nothing like it, having each other like this, with no barriers between us since she went on birth control. I grip her hips with my hands and slam her against me, each hard thrust rocking the Harley beneath us. I'm living a fantasy I filed away ten months ago but the reality is outweighing that fantasy now as we both go over the edge together and she screams her orgasm in my ear as I fill her to the brim with my seed.

It takes us a long time to catch our breath as we kiss softly, our hands touching, lingering, stroking until the fires re-ignite. I lift her, carrying her back through to the bedroom and toss her on the bed.

It's gonna be a long night with this woman of mine. And I wouldn't have it any other way.

Printed in Great Britain
by Amazon